George Washington
His Legacy of Faith, Character, and Courage

Almighty God, and most merciful Father...
give me grace to hear thee calling on me in thy word,
that it may be wisdom, righteousness, reconciliation, and peace....
Grant that I may hear it with reverence,
receive it with meekness, mingle it with faith,
and that it may accomplish in me, gracious God,
the good work for which thou hast sent it.
Bless my family, kindred, friends, and country;
be our God and guide us this day and forever for his sake,
who lay down in the grave and arose again for us,
Jesus Christ our Lord. Amen.

George Washington's Sunday Morning Prayer

George Washington
His Legacy of Faith, Character, and Courage

Written and illustrated by
Demi

Ignatius

The inspiring legacy of George Washington's life is one of faith, character, and courage. It is visible through the many events told in this book. It began even before he was born, with his ancestors who had been involved in key moments in British history. George Washington certainly learned from their stories, as we can learn from his.

is mother, Mary Ball Washington, was descended from John Ball, who in 1381 rode about England on horseback declaring that all men are free and equal. King Richard II had him hanged for stirring up rebellion. But years later, George Washington too would fight to make men free and equal!

On his father's side, George was descended from a certain Athelunold Wassengatone, who, in recognition of his valor, was given land by the Saxon king Edgar in 963. How brave George Washington would also be.

The Norman king William the Conqueror invaded England in 1066. Norman knights were also among George Washington's forebears. His family's ancestral home was built by William de Wessyngton (later, Washington) in the 12th century, and it still stands to this day.

In the 16th century, King Henry VIII closed the monasteries and sold most of their lands. One of these estates later became the home of Lawrence Washington. He renamed it Washington Manor.

Sir Henry Washington fought for King Charles I during the English Civil War, in the 17th century. After the king was defeated and Oliver Cromwell took power, the Washington family lost their fortune. About this time, John Washington, George's great-grandfather, left England for the New World. He went to the Colony of Virginia in 1657, seven years after Mary Ball's family had arrived.

John Washington bought many acres of land along the Potomac River and planted tobacco. He was elected to the House of Burgesses, which made laws for Virginia, and he became a colonel in the colony's militia. His grandson Captain Augustine Washington married Mary Ball in 1730, and they had a son on February 22, 1732. They named him George.

Little George grew up on Ferry Farm in Virginia. There, he learned the skills needed for farming, hunting, and fighting in self-defense. He read the Bible and many great books in his family's large library. His God-fearing and hardworking parents taught him very early that "life is empty without religion" and that "the tree of knowledge is barren unless rooted in love."

When George was six years old, his father gave him a hatchet. He began using it around the farm, and one morning, for no reason, he chopped down his father's favorite cherry tree. When his father asked him about it, young George hesitated but then bravely said, "I cannot tell a lie, I am the one who cut down the cherry tree."

George's father did not punish him but said instead: "Honesty is worth more than a thousand trees. Thank you for telling me the truth."

On another occasion, George's father gave him some cabbage seeds and helped him to plant them in such a way that the cabbages would spell out his name. George was so excited to see the letters emerge from the soil! When he thanked his father for this marvelous garden, his father said, "Never forget: it is your Father in heaven who gives life! He is the one who has made this garden grow!"

GEORGE WASHINGTON

George was only eleven when his father suddenly died. As the oldest child still at home, he had to help his mother run Ferry Farm. And at the age of thirteen, George began copying and memorizing *The Rules of Civility and Decent Behavior*. Written by French Jesuit priests, these rules were meant to train young men to serve God and neighbor. They helped form George's sense of right and wrong, his strong faith, and his upright nature.

One day, George found his father's surveying tools. He studied them and quickly learned how to use them to map unexplored land.

At age seventeen, he became the youngest surveyor for Culpeper County, Virginia. In this unsettled territory, George learned how to survive on the frontier and to recognize the value of good land. In skirmishes with Native Americans, he also learned tactics of guerrilla warfare that would later help the Americans win the Revolutionary War.

Since his father's death, George had looked to his elder half-brother Lawrence for guidance and support. At the age of sixteen, he went to live with Lawrence and his wife, Anne, on their plantation named Mount Vernon. Lawrence was intelligent, elegant, and a brave military officer. He was George's hero, but sadly he became very ill. When doctors said that a warm climate might cure him, Lawrence and the then-nineteen-year-old George sailed to the Caribbean island of Barbados. Alas, Lawrence died a year later. George helped his widowed sister-in-law manage Mount Vernon, and upon her death he inherited the estate.

At the age of twenty-one, George became a major in the Virginia Militia. In the fall of 1753, he was given the dangerous assignment of crossing the Allegheny Mountains to deliver this message from King George II to the French who were moving into the Ohio Valley: "Leave the lands claimed by the British Crown." At that time, the lands in question were part of the Colony of Virginia. After Washington delivered the message and safely returned from his perilous mission a hero, he was promoted to the rank of lieutenant colonel.

A few months later, in the spring of 1754, Washington was sent back to the Ohio Valley to defend it against the French. After a humiliating defeat, he felt duty-bound to resign his commission. But when British General Edward Braddock arrived, Washington volunteered to help him fight the French. In the midst of a terrible battle, Braddock was fatally wounded and ordered a retreat. As Washington rallied the troops, his horse was shot from under him. He found another horse, and, after it too was shot, he mounted a third one. Two bullets went through his hat, and four pierced his coat. Yet Washington remained unhurt and led the British survivors to safety.

Washington did not think this was luck. "By the all-powerful dispensations of Providence," he said of the battle, "I have been protected beyond all human probability or expectation." For his brave leadership, he was put in charge of Virginia's entire military force. Under his command, the militia protected the settlers who tamed the Virginia frontier. In 1758, he and his men helped General John Forbes drive the French from the Ohio River Valley. Afterward, Washington again resigned his commission and returned to Mount Vernon.

One evening at a dinner party, Washington met a beautiful and wealthy young widow. Her name was Martha Dandridge Custis. She owned a great plantation named White House and had two small children nicknamed Patsy and Jacky. George was more than six feet tall, and Martha was barely five, but as they were close in age and similar in background, they made a good match. They were married on January 6, 1759.

George loved Martha for her great qualities. She was dutiful, considerate, graceful, and had simple ways.

George moved his new family to Mount Vernon. With the addition of his wife's estate, twenty-seven-year-old Washington was one of the richest landowners in Virginia.

The British Parliament began taxing many goods sold in the colonies. "No taxation without representation," protested the angry colonists. King George III of England tried to keep the peace by eliminating all the new taxes except the one on tea, but the Americans were not satisfied. In protest, some colonists, including George Washington, stopped drinking tea altogether. When colonists refused to unload the tea from British ships in Boston Harbor, the governor of Massachusetts threatened the use of force.

In response, on the night of December 16, 1773, colonists dressed as Native Americans boarded the British ships. They opened hundreds of chests with hatchets and heaved tons of tea into the ocean. King George was outraged by this "Boston Tea Party," and the British Parliament closed Boston Harbor.

In the fall of 1774, the thirteen colonies sent delegates to Philadelphia for the First Continental Congress. George Washington was one of the delegates from Virginia. The delegates asked Britain to end all unjust laws and taxes. But King George and Parliament were stubborn and refused to make any changes.

On June 15, 1775, the Second Continental Congress met in Philadelphia. They unanimously elected forty-three-year-old George Washington as commander-in-chief of the newly formed Continental Army. This army was the laughingstock of England, for they were untrained, unequipped, and unpaid.

But the great patriot Patrick Henry had recently shouted from the pulpit of Saint John's Church in Richmond, Virginia: "Give me liberty or give me death!" The willingness to fight for freedom had already spread like wildfire throughout the colonies.

General Washington went to Boston, where the Continental Army was trying to pressure the British to leave. He decided to put cannons on a hill and point them at the British fleet in Boston Harbor. But how could he do so without the British noticing? On March 4, a mist descended, and the Americans were able to fortify the hill without being seen by the enemy. When the British realized that their ships were in danger, they retreated. Boston belonged to the Americans!

On July 4, 1776, the Continental Congress signed the Declaration of Independence. The signers placed their trust in God and his Divine Providence as they declared that the colonies were henceforth free and independent states no longer under British rule. They stated their belief that God had created all men equal and had endowed them with the unalienable rights of life, liberty, and the pursuit of happiness.

News of the Declaration of Independence soon spread to New York, where General Washington had moved his troops to defend the city. He had several of his brigades march into town to hear the document read aloud. At the end of the reading, a cheering crowd pulled down a statue of King George III.

The British army, under the command of General William Howe, attacked the Americans at New York. Howe's army was not only larger than Washington's, but also better equipped and better trained.

The British defeated the Americans and took the city. Washington ordered his men to retreat to Philadelphia. Howe thought he had seen the last of them, but on Christmas night Washington pulled off a daring plan. He led his troops across the icy Delaware River in a snowstorm, and the next morning, in Trenton, New Jersey, they took a British garrison in a surprise attack.

A year later, during the winter of 1777–1778, Washington's faith and courage were sorely tested.

His soldiers at Valley Forge, Pennsylvania, were cold and hungry. Many had no shoes; their bleeding feet were wrapped in rags. Others had no winter coats. Overwhelmed, Washington said, "We are nearly finished." He wrote to Congress, begging for more supplies, and he prayed for divine intervention.

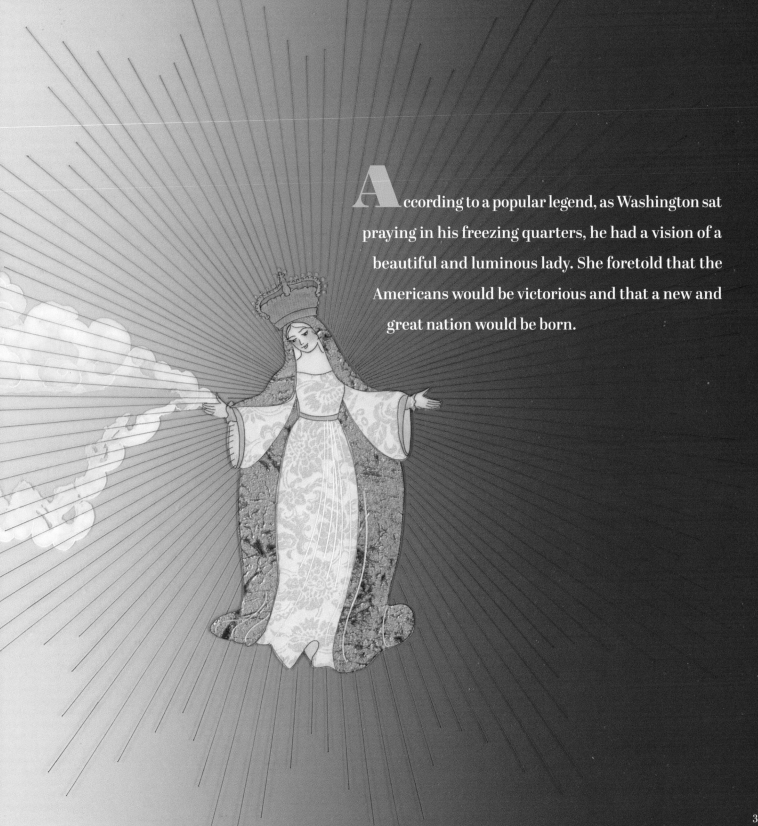

According to a popular legend, as Washington sat praying in his freezing quarters, he had a vision of a beautiful and luminous lady. She foretold that the Americans would be victorious and that a new and great nation would be born.

That winter was the turning point in the Revolutionary War. Prussian military expert Baron Friedrich von Steuben arrived at Valley Forge to train the American soldiers. Later, the French joined the Americans as allies and sent officers, troops, and ships. Washington marched from victory to victory until the Battle of Yorktown, where the British eventually surrendered on October 17, 1781.

Although the war with Britain was over, the peace treaty that recognized the independence of the United States was not signed until September 3, 1783, in France. The last British troops left New York the following November, and Washington celebrated. The grateful country was almost ready to make him their king, but once again he resigned his commission and went home to Mount Vernon. Even the King of England was impressed by his humility!

Shortly after independence was won, individual states began pulling away from the Union.

Washington prayed, "Lord, help us become one." In May 1787, the Constitutional Convention met in Philadelphia to write the Constitution of the United States. Washington chaired the convention, because to everyone he symbolized the spirit of unity. Once the Constitution was approved, he retired again to private life.

His life was not his own for long. On April 30, 1789, Washington was unanimously elected first president of the United States. He took the oath of office on the balcony of Federal Hall in New York. People cheered, church bells rang, and guns fired. In his inaugural address, Washington said, "No people can acknowledge the invisible hand of God more than the people of the United States. Every step towards independence was protected by His hand. Let us remember that the smiles of Heaven will continue on a nation only when it heeds the eternal rules of right and order."

Washington was elected for a second term as president, and, at its end, he delivered his famous Farewell Address. He said, "Of all the dispositions and habits which lead to political prosperity, religion and morality are indispensable supports."

At last, George could finally return to his beautiful Mount Vernon. He had many ideas for improving life on the farm, including an ingenious sixteen-sided barn he had built for threshing wheat. Horses running on the upper level made the wheat grains fall through half-inch gaps in the floorboards to the level below. The wheat was then sacked and taken to Washington's mill to be ground into flour.

37

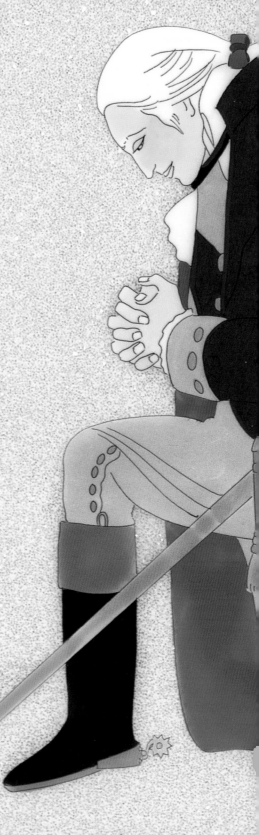

On December 12, 1799, Washington rode out to inspect his farm. It started to snow, which became hail, which turned into a cold, steady rain. The next day Washington woke up with a sore throat, but he refused to take medication. That night he could barely breathe. His last words were, "'Tis well."

George Washington was buried in the family vault at Mount Vernon. Minute guns and cannons fired their final salute. When his will was read, it was discovered that he had freed all of his slaves. He had put into practice the words he had fought for: "All men are created equal." Congressman Harry Lee said he was "first in war, first in peace, and first in the hearts of his countrymen."

Editor, MAGNIFICAT: Isabelle Galmiche
Editor, Ignatius: Vivian Dudro
Proofreader: Claire Gilligan
Assistant to the Editor: Pascale van de Walle
Layout Designer: Gauthier Delauné
Production: Thierry Dubus, Sabine Marioni

© 2018 by MAGNIFICAT, New York · Ignatius Press, San Francisco
All rights reserved.
ISBN Ignatius Press 978-1-62164-234-3 · ISBN MAGNIFICAT 978-1-941709-59-7
The trademark MAGNIFICAT depicted in this publication is used under license from
and is the exclusive property of Magnificat Central Service Team, Inc.,
A Ministry to Catholic Women, and may not be used without its written consent.

Printed in Malaysia by Tien Wah Press in December 2017
Job number MGN18002
Printed in compliance with the Consumer Protection Safety Act, 2008.